Faith WITHOUT FRUIT IS DEAD

KONE MPHELA

Published by Revival Waves of Glory Books & Publishing

PO Box 596| Litchfield, Illinois 62056 USA

www.revivalwavesofgloryministries.com

Revival Waves of Glory Books & Publishing is committed to excellence in the publishing industry.

Published in the United States of America

Paperback: 978-1-68411-074-2

Table of Contents

Chapter 1.

Barack distraught.

A fruitless faith is dead.

Barack grandmother was a sweat, hardworking and prayerful woman, whom Barack adored so much, she was her role model, she admired her grandmother prayer life .They lived in Limpopo North of South Africa in a village called Manoge . Because of lack of education and minimum exposure of the true Gospel of Jesus Christ, Barack grandmother was only exposed to a religion of mount Church lead by a self-proclaimed light of god. He founded his church in the early 19th century while most people were still worshipping idols and he introduced them to God however he wasn't rooted in the word of God therefore he introduced a doctrine which is mixed with their tradition. He was the only bible his church members were reading; they followed him and Barack grandmother was one of them.

As she grows, Barack wondered what kind of religion it was as it was of no help to anyone including her grandmother who was praying every morning and every night yet they still suffer and not even one prayer was answered. She also learnt that it was prophesied at the church that her own parent will

Faith Without Fruit is Dead

not be married for long, and few years later it happened. She wondered if these self-proclaimed powerful man of god who compared himself with Jesus after he has foreseen the separation, why didn't he prevented the separation of her parents, if not for anything but for the sake of Barack father was one of his pastors in his church. Jesus did in John 16:33 he foresaw that his people will face trial and tribulation and he said to his people" be of good cheer for I have overcome the devil and deprive him of his power to harm you," even though the Bishop has help people to denounce the worship of ancestor, he has done little or nothing much to liberate the people from idol worship as they idolized him.

His members knew nothing about the Holy Spirit and nothing about Holy Communion. They use speaking in tongues as a sign to show off to people that they are anointed to become a prophet.

Barack since she was still a child then, she couldn't find the answers she was looking for, neither did her grandmother had them, she just told Barack to stop being inquisitive.

At grade 8 Barack got exposed to Christianity through one of her classmates, she was always talking about Jesus these and Jesus that, while the rest including Barack were talking of Bishop these and Bishop that.

The doctrine of the Christian was different from the doctrine of the mount church, yes they all believed in praying and laying hands on the sick people using three colored piece of paper anointed by the Bishop, and the Christian were praying for the sick in the name of Jesus and taught of fasting and prayer. And when it comes to sexual staff Christians were taught to abstain from sex till they are married, whereas mount church pastor and prophet only taught people not to go to clinic to get contraceptives as it was considered a sin or taboo, yet they said nothing to people concerning adultery and fornication as Christians put it.

Barack found that to be odd and appreciated the teaching of the Christian and she decided to adopt the little she can like pledged herself till she got married, she was even more interested to know more about Jesus, at one time her friend asked her to visit her Christian church so that she can fellowship with them on Sunday, when Barack asked permission from her grandmother, her grandmother refused to let her go and she told Barack to stay away from the church of fashion which glorifies the white man God who does know about the way of life for Africans and their tradition. Barack grandmother was referring to Jesus as the God of white man only; eventually, Barack gave up her quest to want to know more about Christian life and embraced the teaching and instruction of the bishop and pastors of the mount church.

Dream to become medical Doctor was dashed.

Barack was very intelligent, all throughout her primary school to grade 9 she was doing well and getting good marks, in grade 10 she started to experience a lot of unexplained setback on her studies. Her ambition in life was to become a medical doctor and at university to study for medical profession you need to have good marks in mathematics and science in high school, and because of her poor family

Faith Without Fruit is Dead

background she needed good marks to get a full bursary so that she could afford to pay for tuition fees, and she really worked hard .However, at graded 10 her dreams started to fade away.

Every time the test come as usual, she will study and practice math's and science, and in the exams she will answer most of the questions correctly on the exam paper in a way she would confidently believe that she might have scored 80 to 90% as she used to, but to her surprise when the result comes she find that she only scored 20%, she will fight the subject teacher for a remark and as they remark the paper in her presence, she would see that she applied a wrong formal or method on the wrong question, she notice that the answers were correct but on a wrong question on all of them, even the teacher was confused as to what kind of a nerve wreck attacked Barack during the test. Math's teacher knew Barack as a bright student, one of her best however she was surprised to see her do such careless mistakes.

She even asked if there was anything out of the ordinary which was troubling Barack causing her so much stress, her teacher even went to see her grandmother. She find out that other than being poor there was nothing causing stress to Barack as the situation at home was the same as before and that never affected Barack marks even after her parents got divorced.

The teacher thought maybe it was hunger which might be affecting Barack concentration because 2 years ago Barack was caught eating other children left over after break and other children were even calling Barack a dustbin girl. But still

Faith Without Fruit is Dead

she was excellent in her Mathematics and overall performance was never affected, why now the teacher asked herself?, she learned that Barack grandmother was receiving food parcels every month and also Barack was getting food from the feeding scheme at school for needy children, she thought maybe there might be a pressure from other children, she called Barack to find out who might be bulling her or putting her under pressure, she learn that Barack was loved and adored by her friends, she was still a happy girl she always known her to be, no stress was contributing to her absent minded on exams. After few months the teacher decided to give up, but before she gave up on her, she tried one last thing.

As part of the exams preparation she will prepared a class test which its marks doesn't contribute to the year mark but the question are 50 to70% the same as the one on the exams paper. Barack on the class test she would get 90% but when the real test come she would get 10%, at 1st the teacher thought Barack was cheating, on the second class test she sit next to her to see if she was cheating on the class test but to her surprise Barack answered all the questions correctly and got 90% again however 3days later the same questions were on the exam paper of the real test Barack failed horribly.

Eventually she gave up on Barack and accepted the new below average Barack, Barack was also concerned of the new her and she told her grandmother about it, her grandmother took her to church and one prophet told them that there were evil spirit which are switching her marks and to overcome them ,Barack must wash herself everyday with water from the waterfalls mixed with the water from the big river in the province and also use Vaseline prayed for by the Bishop ,it cost Barack grandmother a lot of money to get those items but still the problem persisted.

One Sunday at church a prophet called Barack and her grandmother , the prophet took more than 5minutes making funny sound and also speaking in funny tongues like a lunatic and a lot of screaming and he told them that the Bishop said Barack should confess her sins and also travel alone to wash herself at the Lepelle river –a big river in the Limpopo province- by then Barack was only 15yrs old and she just started to see her period, she was confused as to which sin she has committed, she felt condemned and persecuted for no reason and the thought of going to the big river frightened her even more ,as from her house to the big river was more than 25km ,and there were rumors of a big serial killer snakes which had drowned 3 teenagers girls in the last 3yrs.

It seems like it does that every year and it has never be found as it moves with the river, it doesn't drawn them at the same spot and that year it wasn't reported to have drawn or abducted anyone so Barack feared that, what if it will abduct her because she was a girl and around the same age as the other victims.

She eventually confessed that one time she cooked while she was on her period and is so happened that just after she finished cooking some pastors and the prophet came to visit her grandmother and she shared the food with them and because according to the doctrine of mount church it was a sin for an unclean woman to prepare food for the anointed prophet. Barack confess to that sin and also explained that she wasn't aware that they will come and eat their food, she was only cooking for her family.

She expected the Bishop to save her from the misery she was experiencing on her studies, yet he seemed to be more concern on who was unclean and who was clean.

She found herself on a waterless pit.

Barack hoped to have someone in her life who was more powerful and merciful, who will be willing to deliver her from all her trouble. She told her Christian classmate about everything even the bishop respond, her Christian friend advised her not to go, as she will pray for her and God will make a way for her somehow . Everyday Barack would feel more and more of a need of these man called Jesus her friend told her about but since she wasn't allowed to visit her friend church, She sworn that, should she get a chance to go to university she would find out more about the Christian life.

In grade 10 Barack gave up of science subjects, therefore she decided that she will take bible studies, geography and history as her stream, as they did research on bible study subject Barack stumbled on the story of a woman with an issue of blood who suffered for 12yrs in the book of Luke 8:43 who went to many places for help yet her situation persisted until she learn about Jesus, and she told herself that if only she could touch Jesus she will be healed.

Faith Without Fruit is Dead

Barack identified herself with these woman, as she has done all she could to get help and did all she was told to do by the prophet yet no help and all her dreams faded away right before her eyes. Barack said to herself "as these woman encountered Jesus and her problems went away so shall it be with me, the 1st thing I will do when I get to university I will look for Jesus church because then I can do whatever I want without answering to my grandmother."

Barack was tired of a dead faith, which was like a pit without water, which was just holding her and her grandmother hostage and also rendering them hopeless and miserable.

The worse was when her grandmother had a stroke, her family did all they were told to do so that her grandmother could get well but still she was getting worse and worse and poverty was also escalating because all her grandmother pension which used to help them to survive was now spend on the water, salt and these and that which the prophet instructed to buy. Even when they took her grandmother to the medical doctor, him too was not of much help because he demanded that her grandmother should get a treatment which they couldn't afford and he also told them that she should eat certain food which they couldn't afford.

Barack was desponded.

At school on the bible study period Barack studied Psalm 40 and she read 1-6 she was so intrigued by the verse and she asked her Christian friend, what David meant.

Faith Without Fruit is Dead

She briefly explained to her that David was feeling desponded and grieved. He cried to God, and he was delivered.

Barack felt that she was also in distress, and she identified with David as she was experiencing pain after pain without help, and she was more convinced that this man she longed to know more about whom her grandmother believed he was a god of white people he was more helpful and merciful.

Later on that month, Barack grandmother past on. when people came to offer their condolences ,her friend mother came and as it is a tradition for Christian people to always quotes scriptures to comfort the grieved ,Barack friend mother read Zechariah 9 :11-12 nobody paid much attention to her except Barack and she was captured by the word waterless pit and prisoner of hope ,as she was hearing about them for the second time.

And after the funeral Barack never set her foot in her grandmother church, even though she didn't go to attend the church of her friend, she has sworn never to have anything with dead religion.

Barack delegated her time to study the Bible, but because she wasn't born-again and she was alone, no one to interpret for her, it was just a subject study to her and stories, in grade 12 she got a distinction.

The devil did everything in his power to stop Barack from be admit at university so that she doesn't meet Jesus.

Faith Without Fruit is Dead

Barack seeing that she lost her dream of becoming a medical doctor, she aspired to be a psychologist, at university they accepted her application during the year however because the devil was always on her case when she went to register in the beginning of the following year after her grade 12 result were out. She was told that she wasn't on the system and they didn't even allow her to do late admission as the course was fully booked.

Barack encouraged herself by saying maybe it wasn't meant to be, she went to do self-application at teachers college so that she can train to be an educator, she was accepted the very same day and was given enrollment form, as she was about to register they cut off the line and were informed to come back tomorrow to finalized registration, when Barack went to finalize the registration the following day, she was told they have cut off as they were fully booked, she should come back next year.

Barack was forced to take a gab year and she applied again to university and she was accepted and she also applied for a bursary at department of health and she was called for interview and she did well on the interview and she was informed that they will get a feedback to her next year however it will be best if she register for the course so that once she is called she will be able to produce a proof of registration that proof that she was studying psychology.

In January when she went back to the university the same thing happened and these time her name was there but the there was a mix up with her surname, and so it looked like someone else profile, the admission number, name and address were correct and the rest was not, therefore she wasn't allowed to register.

Chapter 2.

Encounter Jesus at TUT.

Enrolled for marketing diploma.

She was so disappointed and the following day she took a taxi to Gauteng province to do self-application at TUT, fortunately she was admitted the same time however TUT doesn't offer a psychology course and since Barack did general subject in high school, her only option was management diploma. as she was about to enroll for public management course she met Mr. Park who was lecturing marketing 1 to 3 at TUT, he saw Barack marks and was impressed they talked for a while, Barack had distinctions and he encouraged her to enroll for marketing courses as Barack was looking on the brochure she noticed that Marketing course has accounting, business law, economics, and statistic. Barack told Mr. Park that she has never done accounting and economic before and it will be the 1st time in her life doing it, Mr. Park said if she work as hard as she worked in her grade 12 it won't be difficult for her. And they always start with basics so that student would catch up.

He gave Barack enrolment form to enroll and register for marketing and Barack took them and went to register and in one day Barack managed to do everything except accommodation.

She told her friend from home who was in her second year, that she has registered for marketing diploma which has accounting and another subject she never saw before in her life, her friend discouraged her and also advised her to deregister the course and register for public management .she also referred her to people she knew that they have repeated marketing 3 times because they were failing economic and accounting. Barack decided to deregister for marketing the following day however all throughout the night the voice of lecturer Park kept on running in her mind and she convinced herself that the lecturer was right and her friend was wrong and she has no faith in her, beside the course of management was fully booked, which means she will have to go back home again.

Barack the following day she didn't go to deregister. However, she went to queue for campus accommodation, unfortunately she wasn't successful as all the rooms were fully occurred, so she was forced to find alternative accommodation outside the campus.

She looked for two days and on the third day she found a room in block M just behind the campus, it was like 1.2km away from the school, Barack paid the landlord for a month rent and went back home in Limpopo to inform her mother of everything. She stayed at home for a week as the lesson were only starting at the end of January, so after a week on Saturday.

Faith Without Fruit is Dead

Barack carried all her bag back to school and she arrived in the afternoon, only to meet her roommate preparing to go to attend crusade at **Christ based Church** ,since it was a second nature for Christian to invite people to come with them to church she invited Barack to join her ,Barack felt an uneasy feeling inside of her , and also remembered a promised she made to herself 4yrs ago that the 1st thing she was going to do once she is on her own was to find a Christian church ,she was also aware that she needed help from someone powerful if she wants to succeed in her new career and pass accounting and statistic so that she doesn't apply the wrong formula on the wrong question again as she did on math's in her high school.

So she figures Jesus might be the help in the present need as David said in Psalm 46:1, in that spirit Barack went to church that very afternoon.

Prayer for deliverance.

Barack 1st experience in the church it wasn't what she expected. She thought that at church they only read the Bible, pray, and the church was over. Because it was a crusade of total deliverance, the pastor did teach and he started to pray, and in the prayer he was provoking the demons, Barack knew about demons but not manifestation, at school Barack learnt about the story in Mark 5, about the man possessed by legion.

She saw people screaming and fighting the pastor and ushers, they were talking scary and diabolical stories. Barack was horrified as if she was listening to a horror story, the only different was there were no pictures .she heard the devil was confessing and telling people how he destroy people and also delaying their destiny .she also thought that the people who were manifesting were the legions themselves, Barack even run away from the girl who was sitting next to her, because she was talking and moving like a snake, Barack run to the door as she had enough of the horror and wanted to leave.

One usher stopped her from living, Barack fought her and the more she was fighting. The ushers thought it was the devil that was making Barack to be violent so they asked Brother Matt who was ushering as well, Matt caught Barack like he was catching a big flies and he pinned Barack down and begin to pray for her. Barack was vomiting on the floor; she didn't even understand why and also beeping.

She now really wished to leave yet Matt was revolted, he held her with all that vomit and prayed for her deliverance. After a Church, her roommate explained to her what was really happening and why people were screaming and the funny part was, some of the people were making the same sound the prophet in her grandmother church were making and in mount church it was perceived as anointing. And now her roommate she called it a demon possessed.

At night , she recalled that all her life she was told to do whatever those Prophets instruct her to do, if they tell her to go to the river she will go and they say go to the mountain and her grandmother would go and now she had how the devil uses rivers and mountain to hide people destiny. This means she voluntarily handed over her destiny and her dream of becoming a medical Doctor to the demons in the river

Faith Without Fruit is Dead

Her 1st day at church was an eye opener that she was just following the instruction of the devil, and was misguided, she recall reading Hosea 4:6 which spoke about being destroyed because of lack of knowledge, her grandmother didn't know about the bible and the Bishop of the church was the only bible they knew and read, unfortunately he was a blind leading the blind.

Barack 1st Holy Communion.

Barack was determined to learn more, the following day it was Sunday and fortunately, the morning service was more focus on God and Holy Spirit and what Jesus has done, unlike the deliverance service which was more on what the devil has been doing in the people lives.

She learned about the love of Jesus and his finished work, his unmerited and the undeserved righteousness he imparted on us. The message was more graced based and they also partook on the Lord super and that was strange to Barack, she never experienced it in her grandmother church, the bishop on Easter conference he will briefly touch on it but he will say only the pastor should partake as they are also his disciples, like Jesus disciples.

As the usher was passing she looked at her roommate as if she was asking for permission with her eyes and her roommate knotted to say yes you may, and she took the bread and wine.

Luckily that day the pastor read John 6:53-56, which end by saying he who eat my flesh and drink my blood, abide in me and I in him. Barack was happy to learn that and it was comforting to her to know that it doesn't cost anything to have Jesus in her life, all she has to do was a simple thing, to feed on him and drink his blood which purifies her daily, and at the end when the pastor called an altar call for people who are ready to be born again, Barack went and she accepted Jesus in her life.

That very same day Barack also learn another new thing , tithe and offering ,at her previous church there was no tithe and the only offering they were encouraged to give was to assist when the Bishop was travelling, to visit kings or politician in the country and around Africa which was happening quite often, that was the offering she knew, the church and the bishop were financially depending on the items they were selling which has the church logos, that's why the prophet or the lights were instructing people to get and use certain ointment they always insisted that they should buy them at the church shops. People travelled miles and miles to that shop to buy salt and Vaseline because they were instructed to use them to remove bad luck.

After the service, Barack roommate took the opportunity to educate Barack even more about the tithe and the purpose of the envelope she saw inside the offering bag because Barack thought they were for prayer requests. She also read Genesis 14:18-20 where Abram received bread and wine from the high priest called Melchizedek and Abram responded by tithe they also read Hebrew 7 which confirms that Jesus is our Melchezedek.

She explained to Barack that our high priest today is Jesus and by giving him the tithe and offering we are also confirming

Faith Without Fruit is Dead

that we are the seed of Abram because when Abram give tithe to Melchezedek he also received the bread and wine which represented the body and the blood of Jesus.

Barack roommate also educated her of the two types of tithe, the Abram tithe and Moses tithe.

Moses tithe is more of a commandment and they gave their tithe to priest or Levites the grandson of Aron, it was of more of a self-righteous act we read on Malachi as well because they acted as God partner not children ,they will give tithe in order to receive blessing from God and those who didn't give were receiving nothing but curses ,she explained to Barack that since we are under Grace our tithing is more of Abram, he gave to honor God and he gave because he received from God, not to purchase the flood gate of heaven to be opened for him ,as if God has a tollgate and you can only pass if you have tithe but not God will send you back or curse you. But Abraham gave tithe because he has received victory from God.

Barack knowing what it feels like to leave under condemnation and curses, she was glad that her roommate knew more about the new covenant of Grace and the finished work of Jesus Christ.

Barack was fascinated that in less than 24 hours she learn more about Jesus than she did in 18yrs of her life and since there was still an afternoon service, which happens to be the last service of the crusade of total deliverance she was looking forward to learn more.

Faith Without Fruit is Dead

As they were walking back to their room after church, suddenly Barack face was overwhelmed by sadness and tears started rolling on her face because she realized that her grandmother didn't get a chance to know about Jesus before she passed on and she also wondered if she was condemned to hell.

She was illiterate and not exposed much expect to that deceiver doctrine .it would be unfair indeed especially since she saw how devoted and faithful she was and how she prayed endlessly every morning and night to a man who was comparing himself with Jesus, and since he was often performing miracles and doing unexplained thing many were convince that he has inherited Jesus powers.

Barack convinced herself that probably her grandmother was between hell and heaven as she didn't qualify to be condemned to hell but neither did she obtained a passport to enter into heaven called Jesus, in that mindset she was more determined to know more, so that she will be able to share her knowledge with the rest of the family who were still alive including her mom who was sickly and leaving on ten different medicine. Because every time she visits a doctor she was diagnosed with a different thing on top of the ones she already suffering from.

Barack became a devoted born again Christian, and she was also blessed to get a student loan even though she was expected to pay it back later when she starts working, but that was a relief to her.

Faith Without Fruit is Dead

After the class has resumed, Barack learnt about the student fellowship on campus SCF and she went to attend weekly services with them.

Barack met her 1st love and discovered her purpose.

Barack befriended a boy named Dan at SCF , a tall slim, dark-skinned boy from springs township ,who liked to dance so much, because Barack was living outside campus after classes she will sit under a shade next to SCF to wait for 5 o 'clock services and one day Dan went to her to introduced himself to Barack and also asked her where she resides , Barack told him that she live outside campus which happened to be closed to where he once lived in his 1st year as well, he was a second year student studying Auditing degree, he was also a born again and grow up in a Christian home. After the service he offered to walk Barack home as it was late and she agreed, on the way, he will sing and show Barack some dancing moves and Barack will copy him, they didn't have much to talk about expect Jesus and singing, the next service he stood up in the worship time and dance as the worship leader were singing and because Barack wasn't sitting far from him, she stood up and joined him on the dancing floor.

For a while they looked like fools as that wasn't common at SCF then, people were used to clap their hands while sitting or standing in one place. Dan and Barack danced alone until the worship time was over and then they sit down to receive the word and after church Dan walked Barack home again and on the way they talked about how they looked like fools, Dan asked Barack "why she didn't stop and sit down after seeing that no one was joining them and people were laughing at them", Barack said "the one I joined on the dancing floor didn't sit down", they laughed.

Dan told Barack how at his church they used to dance as their pastor taught them how to worship God through dancing and singing and since Dan can't sing even to cheer himself he decided to worship God by dancing like the children of Israel when they were marching\dancing around the walls of Jericho and for a while he wanted to do that but he couldn't, her joining him gave him a courage that's why he didn't stop.

Barack was learning the Christian life, so as long as Dan was dancing she followed, that was how they become a team, and they called themselves BKDan dancing team.

Every day they will dance even though on the social media other student were mocking them and posting their video. Dan and Barack were determined to worship God through dancing.

Eventually, when the music was good, some student would join them, and every time Dan walks Barack to her room they will sing and dance on the road as if they were drunk with other friends.

Dan in his youth service life he was taught to make a church time, a party time so that he can enjoy his youth and not feel like he was missing out on the fun. Because of team Dan and Barack church service become more fun and more student were attracted to attend the service and also to dance on the dancing floor, it was even commented by the visiting pastors who were often invited to preach on Sunday, some of them have been coming to SCF but never experience a life church like that, usually student were all serious or tired, looking like pupils attended a class just to be marked present.

But team Dan and Barack changed that tradition, even the pastor invited the dancing team to joined them at their churches to spiced up their church with their high worship spirit of dancing, it was all fun for Dan and Barack and for other friends who joined the dancing team.

Sometimes they were invited to visit churched far from school, and Barack wasn't able to afford the bus fare.

And when they came back they will come with new dancing moved they also learnt on their trip, and Barack wouldn't know them as she wasn't there.

Then Dan will lead with order people, some girls also befriended Dan and wish that Dan will give them the same attention he was giving Barack and every time Barack was not around they worked so hard to replaced her and showed Dan that they could also dance, and they are also fun to be with.

Dan been just a fun guy he didn't see any harm, after all, they were all dancing to glorify Jesus not themselves and he became their friends but since they were threatened by Barack they always make sure she feels not welcomed in their presence. Barack begins to sense the spirit of competition because they will hurry to ask Dan to walk them to their room even though they were staying inside the campus .and because it would be late to walk Barack home after he walked them, Dan ask some of his friends to walk Barack and the distance between them grew bigger by the day, Barack would mostly leave long before Dan notice that she was around just to avoid the competition.

Barack found comfort in Matt's arms.

One time the trip to go to Durban for a concert was announced and they were invited to spice up the dancing spirit at the concert, Durban is 700km from the campus, the coordinators invited them and also offered a free ticket for the concert and also to subsidies their bus fare and accommodation.

The whole trip after subsidy was R500 including two nights and breakfast and dinner, and the hotel was closer to the beach, most student at SCF even the one who were not member went but Barack couldn't afford and that made her very sad, on Friday around 4pm after all the buses left and she came to see if they were some people who were left to held the service so that she can shake off her sadness.

She stayed under a shade next to the SCF for an hour and nobody came and sadness overwhelmed her and she felt sorry for herself, a few minutes later Matt came.

Matt was a second year engineering student, who came from Mamelodi township which was 45km east of the campus, Matt because of his two exams on Monday he decided not to go on a trip so that he can study, as a leader of the intercessor or prayer team he volunteered to check on the church while they were gone to look after those who didn't make it.

As Matt was approaching he notice Barack sitting under a shade next to SCF, he passed her and she didn't even notice him, she was so downcast and sad, only when she heard the sound of the keys she looked up, the SFC was on the 1st floor and on the ground floor was the school radio station.

Matt opened the door and went inside and stood by the window and looked at Barack through the window hiding behind the blinds. Barack didn't move as she only saw one boy, she stayed there hoping that one or two will come so that they can pray together but nobody came.

Matt also happened to be one of Barack secret admire and he often sit next to Barack in the church service but she never noticed him, he also happened to know some of her favorite songs, seeing that she wasn't the cheerful Barack he knows, he went down to the studio and requested that they play one of Barack favorite song of.. My life is in your hands... by Kirk Franklin, he pleaded that they shouldn't interrupt it and also allow it to play until the end, fortunately DJ that time was someone who also knew Barack from the service and as Matt told him that he was dedicating the song for Barack who was feeling down, the DJ played it after just a few minutes and he did as he was requested.

As the DJ was playing the song Matt approach Barack while singing with it and unlike Dan ,Matt was a good singer, Barack lift up her face and saw these tall, strong good looking man of God who was singing nicely, Matt body was well built , he come from the family of giant man, he looked like he was 30yrs old but he was only 21 and with the glory of God on him people couldn't help themselves around him but to respect him, even the kind of wisdom he has both in church ministry and his studies was extraordinary, he was one of the top students in his faculty.

Barack knew Matt even though she never paid any attention to him; to her Matt was one of the student pastors.

Matt after sang the whole song for her, he sat down to introduced himself and was surprised when she said "I know you ", you are one of the student pastor and a leader of the prayer group.

Matt was enticed, he stared at her for a while and he played the song again from his phone for her and he was again singing with it and Barack started to hammer with the song as well, they stayed there for almost an hour and when he saw that it was 5:45 and no one was coming, he asked if they could just pray together, Barack agreed and they held hands together and Barack hands are not the type of hands any man should be held. They are soft and magical and her eyes and her voice very seductive...Matt giant or no giant he was no match, he remembered the first day he saw Barack at the crusade when he was asked to help with her because of her violent reaction. Barack wasn't all that beautiful, but she was well built as well and had right assets of the African woman, enough to spin the head of any young man with hot blood running through his veins.

As they were praying he noticed she was fighting to hold tears in her eyes, he held her closer and embraced her but in a godly way but either way that was big mistake on Matt because he was attracted to her, Barack wept even more Matt felt for her, but he didn't know how to ask her what was her problems.

After a while she apologized and decide to live and Matt couldn't allow her to live just like that because it was obvious that something was bothering her, he stopped her and asked her to sit down again and tell him what was a problem, she was aware that he was a prayerful man of God, so she to confided in him.

Unfortunately or fortunately she told him how she was also bothered by the reaction of some girls in the church who were sidelining her, she admitted that even though her and Dan were not dating, she sometimes missed just to be with him alone and he was so blinded by popularity, he didn't realize that he has left her far behind.

Matt thought Barack and Dan were dating that's why he kept his distance, just admiring Barack from far.

He was pleased to learn that they were not dating, he asked Barack if she ever thought of joining other teams like intercessors team, Barack said she was new on Christianity and she doesn't know much about interceding let alone pray for herself, and it was only few months since she was a born again.

Matt said to Barack "a successful life of a Christian is also based on his\her prayer life because God works in our life only when we ask him in prayer, that why the Bible says make your request be known to God in prayer and thanksgiving."

Faith Without Fruit is Dead

He recruited Barack to join his team and also had a privilege to walk her home that Friday evening, Matt that night he slept very happy, he fell in love with Barack that night, he kept on feeling Barack hands on him and even her aroma, Barack wasn't wearing any perfume on her but just roll-on yet her natural scent hypnotized Matt.

Matt even called one of his friends who went on the trip, and told him that he not going for a trip was a divine intervention, because he found the love of his life.

His friend was surprised because he knew that Matt was kind of dating Thandi, and she was with them on a trip.

He asked Matt and said, so you finally realize that Thandi is the one, Matt said Thandi who?

I mean the girl I told you about 4months ago, but I couldn't approach her because she was dating Dan, his friend said "ooh you mean BK" .Matt said yah She is not his girlfriend because they are not dating, and they haven't been together for 2months now.

Matt confesses to his friend how much he felt about Barack ever since the day he saw her at the crusade in Faith Apostolic mission church in January.

On Saturday Matt and Barack were together again for prayer session with two other friends of Matt and after that Matt walk Barack again and they spend the rest of the afternoon watching movies on his tablet.

Faith Without Fruit is Dead

at first Barack was uncomfortable sitting so close with a man she just basically met but something in her stopped her from moving she ended up leaning on him to rest her neck and he was too happy to support her, she found Matt to be a pleasurable company. beside the movies they were watching was faith based not that romantic and they were at the park full of other students, after the movie Matt asked Barack to attend Sunday service with him at the local church where they first met.

Matt offered to pick up Barack at her room so that they can walk together.

Sunday morning Matt was at Barack room by 7am, she wasn't even ready then, when Barack saw how he was dressed she fell on her bed, he was looking good on his black expensive suite. She was so intimidated by the way he was dress because she didn't have anything half that good or expensive. She was planning to wear a jean and shirt but looking at him she realizes that would be inappropriate or too casual.

Matt was waiting patiently in the living area, and when he realized that it was almost an hour, and Barack is not coming, he asked her roommate to call her. When her roommate got to the bedroom she found Barack crying and her eyes were all reddish, she quickly went back to Matt and said "I think there is something wrong with BK because she is crying" Matt was surprised because he just saw her an hour ago and she was fine, so they both rushed back to the bedroom and BK was still on her bath towel.

Faith Without Fruit is Dead

Matt asked what happened, and BK said "I think I am not feeling well, so I won't be able to walk with you to church" and she rushed him out of the room.

Matt was confused because Barack was just fine a while ago and now she doesn't even want to see him. He sits on the couch again waiting for her to be dressed again. He didn't want to go to church alone neither to leave her behind like that.

 back in the bedroom Barack told her roommate what was really her problem, so she helped her to choose a nice and simple dress she has and encouraged her to go to church and focus on God not how well she is dressed, Barack said to her roommate "is easy for you to say as you are not the one who will be walking with that center of attention in there, if I was walking alone I wasn't going to bother"

Barack roommate after she has helped Barack to choose a nice dress she left and as she pass the living room she found Matt still waiting and he asked her if Barack was okay and she said "she will be fine ,it was just attire issues but she will be ready soon" Matt asked her what she meant attire issues and she told him that BK was feeling out of place because of the way he was dressed as she didn't have anything these expensive, she touched the color of his suit' Matt felt bad as he worn that suit to impress her not to intimidate her.

After few minutes Barack was done, and they took a taxi as they were almost late and when they arrived dat the church they found Matt two friends waiting for them at the gate.

Faith Without Fruit is Dead

After the church on Sunday, the four of them spend the afternoon together at the park waiting for the buses to return from Durban whiles watching sermons of Dr. Creflo Dollar teaching about the power of praying in tongues on YouTube, when it got late they walked Barack home.

Dan after the trip he didn't give himself a chance to be with Barack and they kept missing each other, and Matt was now walking Barack home after prayer session, on Saturday they were evangelizing together, Matt, his friends and Barack recruited many students to come and fellowship with them and also prayed for many student.

Barack and Matt became very close friends; they spend more time together every day especially on weekend , Dan didn't notice that he has been replaced until one Saturday afternoon at the movie center Matt and Barack came together followed by their friends.

Matt showed his love to Barack.

When Barack was joining a prayer team they opened a file, Matt saw her date of birth and saved it, so that Saturday happened to be Barack birthday and Matt planned a surprise party for her with another team member, he bought her flowers and movie tickets.

When they were done with evangelism, he persuaded Barack to come to watch a movie with him, Barack went to her room for a quick shower, when she come back, Matt was waiting for her at the door of the center, and he gave her the most beautiful flowers and it was her favorite.

Faith Without Fruit is Dead

She screamed and hugged him, she was so happy .she didn't even realized that people were staring, she held Matt hand as they walked to the upper row, she wasn't even mindful of who was looking at her, her eyes were on Matt because she wanted to know how did he find out that it was her birthday because in the morning no one mentioned anything they all pretended as if they were not aware that it was her birthday and she didn't say anything either.

They sat down just 3 rows above where Dan with of his new friends were, Barack didn't even notice that Dan was also looking at her, they watch trailers and advert on the screen and just before the movie started while everyone was attentive, on the screen came dug holding flowers the same as the one Matt bought singing Happy birthday to Barack, Matt stood up 1st and hold her hands, his two other friends followed and the rest of the prayer group on the next row stood up and join Matt to sing for Barack. It was so beautiful and Barack felt very special for the 1st time. Matt seeing that Dan kept looking at the back, he held Barack hands the entire time of the movie. Barack couldn't even eat her popcorn however she was too happy to mind.

After the movie, they went to the church where the party was organized in her honor, she didn't let go of Matt hand, until when Dan called her, Matt felt her letting go of his hands and he grasped her hand back, when Dan was about to hug her, Matt quickly came in between them to hinder Barack and said, Babes we can't enter in there without you please lets go,.

Dan frowned and repeated Matt words to himself and said Babes since when?

Faith Without Fruit is Dead

Dan followed them upstairs at the church when Dan saw the decoration, the cake and big platter of different food, drinks; he was so jealous and left immediately. And the party went on until midnight prayer started, after the prayer, Matt asked one of the girls to accommodate Barack for the night as it wasn't save to walk her home at that time.

On Sunday as usual, Barack came to church an hour earlier for intercession and Dan went to her room to fetch her so that they could walk together to the student center wall where the Sunday services are held, to his surprise Barack was gone already.

Dan only notice that Sunday that Barack was actually no longer dancing with them, she was sitting next to Matt. He also noticed that she was ushering the people Matt was praying for at the time of praying for those who were not feeling well, before the preacher start.

He was confused as to what Matt was to his friend Barack, Dan by then he was already the conductor of the church choir, also a busy man and surrounded by new friends. He let it go on Sunday and planned to see Barack at Library on Monday ,he knew where Barack often sit , therefore on Monday he went to library and he couldn't find Barack and he went to the auditorium where she study at some time , when he got there he noticed Matt was also studying at the same place.

After some time Barack took a break to get a fresh air outside, Dan followed her and offered her water, she accepted and thanked him, for a while they kept quiet.

Dan harshly asked Barack "What is Matt to you?

Faith Without Fruit is Dead

While Barack was about to answer, he interrupted her and said with an anger tone,

"I left you for just one weekend, and you replaced me with that! Dan was pointing in the auditorium, just because he is flashing money on you, I never knew you were so cheap and can be bought with anything money can buy",

Because Dan raised his voice, Matt heard him and went out. Barack was just looking at him with her mouth opened because she couldn't believe his attitude. Dan continued and said "you even compromised yourself and slept with him, sis you are so cheap "

Then He hid Barack nerve, and she lost it.

she said "what on earth is eating you up, you left me for your new friends and for months you never bother to ask if the people you asked to walked me home actually did walked me home safely ,you passed me on like an old piece bread as soon as you met your new friends and when you came back from the trip still you didn't even find it necessary to find out how I was or share with me your experiences at the trip ,I came to your room after week and your room was full of girls ,the same girls whom I once told you that they are treating me like a parasite or unwanted third leg and you didn't even notice that I was there, now you have a nerve of being jealous because I have a new friend too and now you noticed me again, we drifted apart long before the Durban trip and Durban trip was a month ago not last week, your friend made me feel like a dirt ,sponger and you were not there for me and you can't claim that you didn't notice that you have thrown me at the back seat and they were stepping on me .

Now you have some nerve to insult me, and behave like I cheated on you with Matt and we were not even dating.

Then she cried and Dan felt so bad because he abandoned the only true friend who he loved him for him and not because he was popular, the only friend who stood by him and supported his mission even when it wasn't easy.

Matt notices that the conversation was sour; he rushed to rescue BK and embraced her, and asked Dan to let her be.

Dan said "I should what? Leave her for you; in your dreams pal, you are not going to take her, I won't let you"

Matt let go of Barack and come closer to Dan and Dan as well stood up tall they were both ready to fight, Barack went inside the auditorium, took her book and left, when they saw that she was leaving they ran to fetch their books so that they can walk her home, she realized that none of these men is willing to back off and are all acting like jealous boyfriends which none of them was, she ran.

Tuesday she studied in her room. She avoided them for a week and on Saturday Matt went to her room in the afternoon, when he got there he found Dan and his friends. Dan was just there to apologize for his attitude on Monday and for neglecting her all these while.

Faith Without Fruit is Dead

Matt got so upset left without saying a word, Barack tried to run after him, but he kept on walking, so she didn't want to draw attention to herself, she turned back.

On Sunday after church, Barack went to Matt, and he yelled at her too and said she should stop being double minded and decide what she wants or whom she want.

Barack was surprised by his attitude and his words of whom she wants, yes Matt bought her flowers, watch a couple of movie with her, walked her home for the past two months and contributed to her birthday party surprise, but that doesn't make him her boyfriend either especially since he also never said anything.

To Barack, they were just her close male friends, who have taught her so much about faith.

It became obvious that they both develop feeling beyond friendship and hoped for more, yet none of them had the courage to disclose his feelings to her.

It was almost toward the end of October, and final exams were around the corner, she decided to focus on her study and worked hard so that she doesn't fail anything, so far she was doing well and even qualified to write final exam even for accounting.

Dan remembered how Barack brought a bit of fresh air and courage in his life and also Matt knows that he was at his best every time Barack joined him on evangelic mission, Barack had these character in her of bringing out the best in these two man and Dan realized that he has missed up and now there was a competitor who was not letting her go

Dan started to turn down Sunday dinner invitation from other girls as he noticed that he almost lost his friend because of it and the popularity become too much and almost took his focus of whom he was actually dancing for which was Jesus.

After the exams, Barack applied for the temp job of helping with the registration at the beginning of the following year, and she got it.

Chapter 3

Grace revolution.

Matt at Barack village.

Around the 15th December Matt called Barack just to find out if she found a church she can fellowship and also requested the phone number of the pastor, it sounded weird but she gave him.

Matt called and convinced Barack local pastor to allow him visit his church and spend Christmas with them, because Barack once told her local pastor about all what she learned from Matt leadership as youth and intercession leader, out of curiosity the local pastor accepted Matt request.

Matt booked himself in a B&B next to the church which was also just 7km away from Barack home; he took his Dad car and head to Limpopo, in his heart he planned to spend his birthday and Christmas with Barack, Matt birthday was on Christmas day, his family usually celebrate his birthday in Cape Town and since he was turning 21 years old ,his dad thought he was going to ask for a big party so he already saved the money for him ,and he was surprised when Matt said I am going to have a party but a different one and I am not even going to holidays with you, because I have a future in Limpopo and I need to go and learn more about it, his dad thought since Matt was an engineering student and Limpopo is full of undeveloped areas he found a project which he was working on and he needed funding, so he gave him all the money which was close to ($1000 USD).and the keys of his brand new Amarok truck because the roads in Limpopo villages are not good.

He arrived on Saturday of a week before Christmas around 2pm because he 1st drove his family to the airport .he checked in at the B&B ,fresh -in up an hour later he went to meet the pastor and introduced himself, and told the pastor all that he learned about his village from Barack that's why he decided to come and see for himself., the Pastor welcomed him and around 5pm Barack came for afternoon prayer service with her home friends, they noticed a beautiful truck at the church, they even touched and prayed that one day God will bless them with cars like that. Matt was standing with the Pastor, Barack noticed the pasture of the giant boy standing with the pastor, it looked familiar, and when Matt turned she ran to him.

Gift of no condemnation to a single mother or divorced women.

Pastor now realized Matt motive was to spend time with Barack, after prayer Matt drove Barack home with her family who were already converted and accepted Jesus as well except her mother. He had dinner with them; it wasn't fancy but because Barack was the good cook the foods were delicious and he left around 10pm. In all that time he was with

Faith Without Fruit is Dead

Barack's mother, who was sharing with him her life story and what lead to her separation from her husband. And how she is avoiding associating herself with the born gain's or even attending their church because of the way they are treating the divorce women .How they like to create group of woman club and in these group, they prefer only married woman and widows. She told him how they treated her like Ebola one time she attended their woman conference. Barack's mom said she would like to follow Barack faith, but her marital status doesn't favor her to be part of them. These group of women are too quick to judge and condemn single mothers and divorced woman as loss woman, they were always reminding them how God hate divorce and adulterous who had children out of marriage, so it wasn't easy for single woman and divorce woman to accept the gift of righteousness because they didn't believe that someone who hate them so much, can give them a gift of right standing before God unless they first sort out their life which is impossible in most cases.

When Matt heard he revolted, he looked at Barack's mother face, he saw sadness and loneliness and the Spirit of God reminded him about the scripture of John 8:11….where Jesus said neither do I condemn you.

Matt explained this scripture in a way in which Barack's mom was no longer feeling condemned, he said " there was a woman who was brought to Jesus to be condemned because he was accused of been adulterers as according to the Law of Moses such people are to be stone to death and they expected Jesus to condemn her however he spoke grace words to her but he called out the sin of her accuser and one by one they left her alone ,which is what I am bringing to you

Faith Without Fruit is Dead

the good news that Jesus doesn't condemn you neither do God hate you because Jesus took all that hate and condemnation upon himself for you, even for the single woman Jesus showed himself to Samaritan women who had five husband , she too was like you ,afraid to mingle with other women because they scorned her but Jesus revealed himself by his father's name I AM. in John 4:26 which he never said that to most people even his own disciple but he did to her ,he wanted her to know that he knows all about her yet he still choose to reveal himself to her ,he told her everything about her , because as people we never know how much we are loved until the person who declare love to us knows everything about us especially our fault ,our sins and shortcoming yet he or she still declare how much they love us with all our fault and even more willing to take our fault and be punished for it instead of us", as Matt was illustrating those two stories to Barack's mom, God spirit was putting it together for her from the inside in its content perfection. She was happy that she had a talk with him because she was almost robbed of her salvation because of quilt and condemnation and Matt lead her into a prayer of salvation, Barack mom accepted Jesus and was saved that evening.

In the morning or should we say in the middle of the night around 12am the Pastor called Matt and he asked him to preach in morning service, Matt said" to him I haven't prepare anything ,neither am I a pastor ,I am just a youth leader at my school leading only 20 people at SCF."

The Pastor said, "I have been praying for God to give me direction for these coming week crusade and ever since I met you, my spirit kept telling me to ask you to preach, so you ask

Faith Without Fruit is Dead

God what he is prepared for us through you, good night Matt we will talk again in the morning" the pastor dropped the phone.

Matt called Barack and told her what her Pastor just said. Barack said "I also felt the same thing yesterday but it wasn't my position to say anything, I am grateful that the pastor listened to God spirit and asked you, I have been trying to share with my people the grace-base faith I learnt from you and It wasn't coming out alright, because there was these negative voice in me challenging me because I just got born again and who told me what I learnt was the truth. So I gave my Pastor the DVD's and Books of the grace based teachers you introduced me to.

So if he asked you to preach, that means he is willing to adopt, be confidence I have seen you doing it many times, the way you do the evangelic is not the way others do, you go around telling people how God feel about them and his unmerited love for them, not what he expect them to do first before he can forgive them, that's why people found it effortless to follow God, and not ashamed of what they are and completely trusting what God is to them. And my people need that ,the youth in my village need to hear and unadulterated grace message and not the balanced one, my Pastor tried but he stumbled and end up mixing the law and grace and it tasted bitter and more confusing gospel."

Matt said "BK to be honest with you I just came here to spend time with you and celebrate Christmas and my birthday with you without any interruption from Dan or anyone,

Faith Without Fruit is Dead

besides I am not a Pastor neither do I aspire to be one, not now anyway maybe when I am 50yrs old."

Barack said "but at school you preach every week and every Saturday you go around compass teaching people about the love and unmerited favor of God to them, many even call you a Pastor.

Allow God to work out, what he had worked in through the preaching of Pastor Prince and Dollar whom you watch every day, the Bible clearly talks about how to work out our salvation, and you once told us what it really meant to work out our salvation.

We are still surrounded by prophet of doom which still preaches do good get good and do bad get bad message.

I am confidence that you can work out the salvation God has worked in you."

Matt said "now I know how Jonah felt when God send him to Nineveh town and why he preferred to go somewhere else. What am I going to do if the people in your village or church rejected me and start living, won't the same Pastor blame me for closing down his church"?

Barack said "then we will all know that they are not ready yet, and if they are not ready to hear the grace gospel, therefore there is no need for my Pastor to open the doors of his church for them, the church is better of closed."

Barack after the phone conversation with Matt, she woke up and starts praying in tongues, with her village and Matt

Faith Without Fruit is Dead

fears in mind she asked the Holy Spirit to help her make a straight to the point prayer for both as she has only a few hours before is dawn.

She knew that if the youth in her village will learn more about unmerited favor of God and believe right ,it will help them to live right – Like Joseph Prince taught of the power of right believing-and they will be able to break free from the spirit of bondage and bad luck.

Sunday morning service God took over Matt ,he preached graced based message and the people were amazed even the Pastor , Matt illustrated Paul letters so skillfully ,as if Joseph Prince or Creflo Dollar was on the pulpit ,he even run out of time, continued on the afternoon service. The local Pastor was stunned, he thought maybe Matt was going to put up a show and start prophesying or freeze but instead he was peaceful and calm, making a lot of sense and revealing a lot of grace and Christ truth in each and every scripture he touched, it was more like a bible study, Matt focus was about Jesus and his finished work.

Many souls were delivered and born again, the local pastor decides to hand over to Matt the whole week crusade he planned and prayed that God will take over again.

Barack and her brother recorded every sermon and every time Matt watched it he was astonished as to who that person was .all he did was to watch one or two sermons of Pastor Joseph Prince and also of Dr. Creflo Dollar, there rest God took over, it was the most beautiful and powerful week that congregation had in a long time, Matt didn't perform an miracle in the church but many miracles happened to people when they arrived at their respective homes.

Matt instead of spending more time with Barack, he spends it with the Pastor and other leaders of the church, he was ten years young than the Local Pastor, but he treated Matt like his old friend and he didn't want to let him go.

Matt spends almost 200$ USD of his own money each day on food for the congregation lunch and dinner, but it looked like he was spending 2000$, food were enough for all the 500 people who came every day. The church members used to be 38 people but since the Sunday Matt started to preach it multiplied every day, at 1st the Pastor thought that people came because of free food but on Wednesday he noticed even the late comers, came early and the one he knows that they always sleep while he preached were awake, feeding on every word Matt was teaching about Jesus.

He was inspired, by Matt teaching, even the way Matt dealt with the people who were criticizing his teaching, they called it lasciviousness preaching which only a youth leader will preach because he wants to encourage other people to have a lazy faith, he was misunderstood by many preachers around the village, they even attended the afternoon service because they wanted to find out, how he was making the money he was donating to buy food.

Matt was teaching about tithe and offering, the tithe of Abraham not the one of Malachi 3:10 which make God promises to look conditional. Matt since he didn't consider his services a church service but bible studies he never once ask for offering or tithe but people gave willingly and thankfully.

At 1st the local pastor thought it was because people got bonus so they have enough to give but soon realized that they gave out of love , he never saw so many happy faces, some people were healed without being prayed for ,another woman who had swollen face and had gone to many places seeking helped ,she attended one afternoon service participated on Holy Communion which Matt asked everyone including children to partook in the lord super whether they consider themselves saved or not. Matt explained that even Jesus disciples were not saved at the time they had the Lord Super because Jesus was not crucified yet at the night he gave them the Holy Communion ,Jesus gave them his flesh and blood to always remember him and not their sin , they whole church partook on Holy Communion everyday ,she went home the following day her face was clean and back to normal, another man who had up normal   stomach   he was   also cured, they told all those testimony to Local Pastor and when he told Matt that there were people who wanted to stand up in the church service to testify about the power of God, Matt refuse to publicize their testimonies least the people misunderstood him again, he said "I am not a preacher but I am just teaching your people what I also learned ,what God decide to do in them is his assignment not mine therefore I will not share his glory."

Many Pastors criticized Matt, why he was giving children and unsaved people the Holy Communion. Matt asked them questions and said, "what does the bread represent?"

Faith Without Fruit is Dead

And they were foolish enough to answer and said the body of Christ.

Matt:

Which we eat it for?

Pastor 2:

For our sickness as the bible said by his stripes, we are held.

Matt:

Laughing, so you are the only one who get sick and your children they never get sick huh?

Pastor 2:

Scratched his head.

Matt:

So what about the blood?

Pastor 3:

For the forgiveness of our sin. Meaning children have no sin.

Matt:

Please don't give me, I heard a child of two years cursing .because we are all born of Adam therefore we are all born with the inheritant sin from Adam and Eve.

Faith Without Fruit is Dead

Besides the Blood is not only for the forgiveness of sin but also for his life, because our life is in our blood therefore for his life in exchange of our life.so that in him we may have life and life in abundance.

Power of praying in tongues.

To have 100 members in that village it was a big achievement, to have 500 including old people was a miracle. Another old lady whom her brother went missing when he was 17yrs old and never came back and out of love for him she named her only son after her missing brother and it happened that him too, her son went missing when he turned 17yrs old. This woman attended Matt services and also participated on Holy Communion on Monday and she was one of those who only came for free food, so when she got home, she said to herself if truly the God of this boy Matt is almighty God and he can do anything anytime as he claimed that his God control time, then I challenge him to bring back my son and my brother to come home to spend these Christmas with me. And she went to bed, but before she slept she imitate Matt prayer as he was praying in tongues, she prayed in tongues for while then she slept.

In the morning she prayed again in tongues while bathing to prepare herself to go to church to eat free nice breakfast, she even laughed at herself as she had no idea of what she just said or prayed for . She didn't understand much about tongue, in her church which was the same as Barack late grandmother's church, they didn't learn about tongues.

Faith Without Fruit is Dead

Barack was always serving breakfast at 8am till 9am just before the service of 9:30am and the local pastor and his wife they thought once people eat breakfast they won't stay for the service that's why they were against Barack serving breakfast before the service but Matt said the food shouldn't be served conditional or as a reward for attending the service whoever will choose to stay let them stay whoever lives after breakfast he or she is welcome to do so, free means free.

So this old woman happened to set next to Matt when she was eating and she told Matt as well about the story of her son and brother, Matt educated her about the power of the naming the children after other people and its ability to carry the generational curses if one is not in Christ but Matt assured the old woman that since she is now in Christ the curse will be broken. the old woman said to Matt but I am not sure if I have accepted your God I just came for food and as long as you are cooking I will come, Matt said is okay with me, the fact that you are here is more than enough. While they were talking a boy of nine years came running, to call the old woman and she insisted of knowing why they were calling her , the young boy said to her ",there is old man by the name of Tharane who said he is your brother is at home waiting for you"

The old woman fell from her chair and Matt helped her to stand up and also drove her - home, when she got there she recognized him even though he was old and worn out, she started shandaring and praying in tongues, Matt was surprised to hear her praying in tongues.

He even laughed because in his head her word of saying I don't believe in your God yet was still fresh in Matt mind.

Faith Without Fruit is Dead

Matt stood there watching her going around the house praying in tongues and also saying "I am changing my son's name, he is no longer Tharane, he is now Peter because upon him God is going to build his temple". Matt laughed even more and loader, instead of the old woman to be offended by Matt laughter, she said pastor you are laughing good because laughter and salvation have finally come to my house, she was no longer calling Matt young man, the old woman was now referring to Matt as the pastor, an hour ago when she was eating breakfast she called Matt a young man.

She was praising God, she didn't even let her brother to talk, and her brother was thinking maybe she was going to be angry with him or reject him. instead, she was overjoyed, when Matt was living because it was almost 9:10 am the old woman drag her brother and directed him to enter into Matt car and said after church we will sit down and talk but now I am ready for Jesus, she also accepted Jesus that morning and she shared her testimony with anyone who cared to listen in her village and among her family and relatives.

It turns out that the time she was declaring that she was changing her son's name from Tharane to Peter, the chains were loss on her son as well and the curse of the name was broken, and he also came home on Friday.

The story of her son was, when he turned 17yrs and completed his grade 12 he went with his friend to celebrate and one of his friend was from another country so he went with him to see his country and at the border they found drugs and the policy of that country on drugs was very tough and because Tharane now known as Peter had no

Faith Without Fruit is Dead

identification on him he was confused as one of the drug dealer and he was sent to jail without trail. Only on Tuesday at about the same time his mother was changing his name, one of the commissioners who was just transferred to that prison recognize the name of the dealer Peter was confused to be, he was surprised that he was there as that dealer was arrested 2yrs ago and he was the one who arrested him and that dealer case was one of the cases that made his career to be where he was .so he asked that he should be brought to him and when Peter arrived he asked, why did they brought the boy to him instead of the man he asked for , they said that their record showed that that was him , and he realized that they had detained the wrong man for 5yrs.

he ordered the immediate release of Peter the same day on Tuesday and the fact that Peter came home on Friday was because they were still negotiating with him an out of court settlement and offered him 5 million Rand payout.

Matt plans to make Barack fall for him worked.

Matt on Christmas handed over to local Pastor and tried to fulfill his own mission which he really came to that village for.

He drove with Barack around to other villages closed to Barack village, at night they stop at a remote place.

Matt told Barack how he wanted to be an astronaut at some point; he find stars fascinating .he pulled over and they sit at the back of his VW Amarok, there was a small mattress and two blankets.

Faith Without Fruit is Dead

He climbed first and stretch out his hand to help Barack to climb, when she saw the mattress and blanket she froze, in her mind she thought that was it, That how she was going to lose her innocent, at the back of a truck in the middle of nowhere.

She looked around, and it was dark and 45km away from home, no car was passing at that time, only the sound of a hyenas and owls.

Because Matt was not planning to do anything to her, when she looked around he thought he was scared of the dark and wild animals.

He said "are you scared? Does this place have dangerous wild animals?"

Barack said, "I don't think so but maybe snakes and hyenas."

Matt said "relax those animal will not climb these truck neither will they fall from the sky. I just want us to observe the falling stars."

He started telling Barack about his childhood dream of becoming an astronaut and educating her about meteoroids.

He covered Barack with blanket so that she shouldn't be cold as she was shaking and he made her lean on his shoulder, by then they have already seen 3 falling stars.

When Barack realized that he was not into sex but just wanted to watch the space with her and admire the stars and the moon, she relaxed.

Faith Without Fruit is Dead

But all of sudden she started to have these burning feeling inside her, as she described it she said "it felt like she just drank a hot sauce and she can feel it moving inside of her and burning everywhere inside of her.

Her heart was pumping faster and louder than usual as if she might have a heart attack. She even feared that Matt could hear it. For a while, Matt was talking but she didn't hear anything he was saying, he thought she was listening to him because she often turned and look into his eyes however she wanted to see if he heard the sound of her heart.

She said to herself "is this how love start and what is with the burning feeling moving up and down inside of me. What is happening to me?"

Matt was going on and on about meteorites, planet Mars, moon rock, Barack didn't hear what come after those names, she was burning inside, holding him tights as if he was ice or water which will quench the fire inside her, she pretended as if she was feeling cold, she thought she will cool off but it get worse, she even thought of ripping his clothes off.

Now she was not afraid of been raped but afraid that if she doesn't snap out of it ,she is going to rape him ,however the Christian part of her said "these is a man of God I can't do these to him ,I can't be the cause of him falling from grace and losing his anointing .beside he never said anything about having feelings for me ,no no no, I can't bring shame to myself like these and she slapped herself so hard ."

Faith Without Fruit is Dead

Matt was surprised to see her slapping herself so hard and "said what did you do that for?" and he massaged her where she hit herself.

She said she heard the sound of mosquito flying almost into her ears, so she was trying to kill it unfortunately in war there are always some casualty even a war against mosquitos .they both laughed.

At least that distracted Barack from her lustful thoughts, and she started sharing with Matt what her grandmother taught her about falling stars, how she was taught to always curse back at the falling stars because they were believed to be a sign of evil.

Matt laughed out, so loud even the creatures in the forest wake up. He said "so we are basically watching the devil working huh, don't worry he can't come to us, if he tries mxm I will fix him.

Barack said "Mr. Fixer are you Oliver Pope now" Matt said no I am Rolan himself Oliver's father. Even the chief of staff knows that he has no authority over me. They were talking about the drama series of the "The Fixer".

Barack said what if this is the Wrong Turn and the serial killer is about to butcher us with an Axe?

Matt said relax I told you who I am; enjoy the nice view of the stars in these clear sky.

He was having a time of his life with the woman of his dreams next to him. Her warmth and vibrating body next to

Faith Without Fruit is Dead

him felt much, much better that any sex he ever had before he got born again. He felt how tights she was crimping him and pretended as if he wasn't feeling anything, he also did notice that Barack didn't hear most of the thing he was talking about and he took comfort when she caresses him. Even though he didn't react, which he wanted so bad but he manage to control himself, he knew that the mission was accomplished, he got her to fall in love with him and to be comfortable around him and to touch him on her own.

After the moon was out, they stayed for a while until the moon brightened the forest. Matt started to talk about the moon and how is the only natural satellite of the Earth; again he was talking to himself as Barack was dreaming about their wedding and their honeymoon in space. Matt realizes that now it was becoming too dangerous for both of them because he might lose self-control and he didn't planned to take it that far. He took her home.

The devil was so mad but not as mad as the people of the ST Mount church, Barack late grandmother church, as most of the new member were from St Mount church who were also tired, of what Paul in the bible called it **"faith without work is dead"**.

Matt taught how Paul meant it when he said faith without work is dead, Matt share with them the way Ps Joseph Prince, Joel Osteen and Dr. Creflo Dollar taught, those 3 are Matt and Barack favorite Grace and Hope preachers.

The local Pastor decides to follow Matt footsteps and even planned to go with TBN to Israel where the guest speaker was

Faith Without Fruit is Dead

Joseph Prince and Matt sponsored the trip as it was expensive in Rand's and the Pastor didn't have enough for himself and his wife then.

And now his church had been growing strong and especially with youth, many drop out student went back to university the following year, Matt and Barack helped them to get the student loan which Barack was using to pay her own tuition fees, as it was paying for everything including her monthly allowance, which out of it she was helping her mom back home to feed her siblings.

Addict where delivered by observing Jesus, no one prayed for them neither did they fast for 30 days, by just observing Jesus and believing right, and believing that they are the righteousness of God in Christ Jesus and confessing it daily.

After Matt trip when he got home he was so astonished ,about what God just did through him, but he begged God not to make him a preacher yet , he can share his grace experience with people but not a full-time ministry .he asked God to help him marry Barack the following year.

He even bought a ring and also told his Dad about it and also Barack local pastor and they both told him the same thing, which was! Wait and pray about it 1st.

Matt is a great man of God, but he had his weakness, the same as David which lead David to sin and kill Uriah. But God wanted to protect both Matt and Barack from that sin.

Barack was just 19yrs old, when Matt intended to engage her, he told himself that he would wait for her to complete

Faith Without Fruit is Dead

before they get married and God saw a big sexual temptation coming their way, so he delayed the answer.

In January the following year Barack went to school early to start with her job. in her heart as well she had burning desire , she fell for Matt so bad she was even dreaming about him but the bad part was, the dream always end the same way, with her in bed with Matt before they got married.

she convinced herself that Matt won't allow that to happen before they got married, she was counting on Matt ability to control himself but God didn't find that strength in Matt when it comes to Barack, the Lord was willing to join them together but couldn't afford them compromising themselves as the devil wanted to destroy their faith through condemnation and quilt.

Instead of Matt telling Barack that he was praying for her so that God will bless them, he kept it to himself and kept his distance from Barack to avoid temptations.

Barack misunderstood it as a rejection; she thought since he came to see her home, he became less interested and attracted on her ,as it wasn't what he expected.

The more Matt kept her at arm's length, the more devastated she got .she thought Matt   might have learned something about her which turned him off, toward the end of February it was obvious that Matt was preoccupied and avoiding Barack at all times, he never wanted to be alone with her, simply because he didn't trust himself but Barack thought he was no longer interested.

Faith Without Fruit is Dead

She even went to his room hoping that he will open up and tells her what is it that she did wrong, but Matt was so quick to walk her out of his room because he was alone with her in his room. He didn't want to engage on heart to heart talk with Barack as it might lead them into demonstrating how they feel about each other.

He really wanted to do right by her and also to keep the focus on God who seemed to have taken a vacation as far as Matt was concern. He was quit on him; he talked to him about anything except the issue of him proposing to Barack. Matt could see in her eyes that she was in love with him, and she was so vulnerable and willing to discuss anything just for them to be together again.

On the other hand, his blood was boiling, unlike Joseph at Potiphar's house when he runs away from Potiphar's wife sexual advances.

Matt couldn't feel his legs so he couldn't run beside they were in his own room where could he ran too. All he could do was to walk her out and he pushed her towards the door, giving her some lame excuse.

Barack went to her room crying and on Sunday she didn't come for prayer meeting, she even came late to church and gave an excuse of having flu; her eye was red.

From the distance Matt saw that she has been crying all he wanted to do was to hold her but something in him kept saying you will get a chance to hold her your whole life but not now.

Faith Without Fruit is Dead

Dan finally realized that Barack was alone and available again, he started to visit Barack, as he heard that she wasn't well he went to her room to see her, he found her and sobbing, when she asked her what is wrong .Barack told him how she made a fool of herself to Matt.

Matt find out about it and he got worried as he knew they have history and Dan wasn't over Barack. Matt planned was to propose before Easter which was at the end of March, two weeks in March Dan asked Barack to be his girlfriend Barack thought maybe to get over Matt was to open her heart for someone else to fill the void Matt left in her; therefore she agreed.

Dan nominated someone to be the leader of the dancing team and also the choir, he told his friends that, he was planning to spend as much time with Barack and rebuild their friendship, both Matt and Dan were on their final year but Matt only had six months to finish as he was semester course and Dan was doing a year course.

Dan proposed to Barack.

While Matt was praying ,Dan decided to be more pro-active, one Friday he pulled Barack out of the prayer meeting , it was around 7pm and he they sit on the most beautiful part of the garden Dan said "now that Matt has other plans for his life and is evident you are not part of it and you said so yourself ,would you please give me a chance again to proof myself to you that I mean well for you and I value your friendship more than any other friendship ,may you be my... and he pause"

Faith Without Fruit is Dead

Barack was shaking " Dan said why are you scared ,I won't take you to bed relax neither I am going to say marry me, not yet anyway relax ,is me Dan your 1st friend don't be scared, he pulled her closer to himself and hold her tightly, I just want you to be my girlfriend   .let's see what will come out of it ,but I need to be the only male friend you have, no more Matt or anyone ."

Barack was relieved to hear that Dan just want to be a boyfriend nothing more as she wasn't sure that she was over Matt. Unfortunately, where they were next to the path, Matt uses to go to his room. Dan made Barack to sit on his lap.

On the way Matt was talking about Barack and asking what happen to her because she just disappeared before the service end, and his other friend said, I think I know where she disappeared too and he was pointing at her.

When Matt saw her, he tripped over nothing and his friend caught him. He couldn't believe his eyes, he went to them and said shouting, BK what is these? .Barack stood up quickly like a thief got in the act from Dan lab but Dan pulled her back, and he gave her a passion kiss while Matt was watching.

Matt felt like sword just split his heart in two, he couldn't believe what he was seeing. Matt went to his room; unfortunately his room wasn't far from where Dan and Barack were so he was able to see everything they were doing. It was a party of two as they were dancing and singing, even when the lawn irrigation system was drizzling on them, they didn't care Barack was so happy.

Faith Without Fruit is Dead

Matt was a kind of man who takes his time to do something, but he can't handle rejection, the whole night Matt was just overwhelmed by self-pity and sadness.

He called his father at around 12am midnight, he told him that he lost the best thing that has ever came in his life to another man, his dad comforted him, and "told Matt that he shouldn't lose hope as engagement is not a marriage; God can still turn the situation.

Matt refused to be comforted; he kept saying that he was not good enough to get a good thing, as usually what he wanted in life kept being given to someone else not him.

In the past −when Matt was still at high school he was one of the best students , so he was nominated to participate on one of the projects which was sponsored by an American engineering company which promised that the winner of the project will get a scholarship to study in America and Matt wanted it so much and he worked so hard with his dad and their project was the best however one student came with one of the best of the best ,so the scholarship was awarded to him and that de-motivated Matt so much in such a way that even his grade 12 was affected and he couldn't even win the local scholarship consequently he gave up on his dream of engineering , he wanted to became a musician because at his family church, he was playing the piano he tried to connect with people who are connected in the industry and for while their promises will look promising but after some time he will lose those deals to someone else ,so he really hated to be a second best because second in his book they always lose. He even took a break of 3years before he gets it together and went back to school to do his engineering diploma.

It turn out that, That model which he made for the project another company after 2yrs came by and offered his dad enough money for it and also a full scholarship, his dad as he was working as an engineer but he wasn't as good as Matt he asked for opinion from some of his friends about the offer and they advised him to opened a business for Matt so that ,that model will create a good profile for Matt and also pave a way for Matt to be well established since that wasn't the only model Matt made, that's when MattMathe engineering consulting PTY LTD was established and registered and because it was born out of Matt brain baby Matt dad made Matt the majority shareholder , that's when a year later he went back to school. He didn't get to go to America however he went to TUT to meet Barack

Both Dan and Barack were well known in the church and around the school and people also know the 3rd wheel called Matt because if Barack wasn't with Matt, she will be with Dan, sometimes with both of them even on study times they studied together.

It was common for every couple who got engaged or started dating to inform the SCF leaders and also to be blessed at the church on Sunday service.

Dan informed the executive of the SCF, and it was announced that Dan and Barack have decided to take their friendship to another level.

Faith Without Fruit is Dead

It also happened that it was Matt turn to preach that Sunday which means he was going to be the one who have to bless Dan and Barack. It was very hard for him to bless them.

He even jokingly admitted that Dan outsmarted him, he also said that Barack is a kind of girl a guy only meet once in his life, after saying that he pause a bit as those words went right back at his heart. Matt didn't stay for long after praying for Dan and Barack, he left and since people were on the party mood, nobody noticed except   Thandi, who was always behaving inappropriately around Matt, she followed him to his room.

Matt was devastated and also having a mixed feeling of blaming Barack for choosing Dan over him after everything they have been together especially in December, so that girl offered him a shoulder to cry on which led to her offering herself.

Fortunately Matt wasn't that weak around her like he was with Barack so he was able to resist her but he didn't kick her out of his room which was his big mistake again because at the party Barack was uncomfortable with the way Matt left and the pain she saw in his eyes when he was blessing them it wasn't easy for her to ignore so she thought of going to his room one last time to iron thing out with him.

She thought maybe she was wrong about Matt losing interest on her after he saw her family.

On the way to Matt room Barack was rehearsing how she was going to apologize to Matt and, she even said to herself that if Matt won't accepted her apology and insist that she made mistake by accepting the proposal she was going to call it off, she really respected Matt opinion and she was still in love with him.

She finally arrived at his door , out of anxiety she was even sweating .When she knock ,the voice of a woman responded, she knocked again because she thought is the person next door mistaking for knocking on her door, again a woman responded ,Barack opened the door and there they were on a bed together half naked both of them , a half-naked woman on Matt bed, she couldn't believe her eyes, she was voiceless , she couldn't even greet them ,she just stood there looking at Matt who just looked at her once and turn away.

She runs out of Matt room to Dan's room, getting there she was crying as if she found Matt dead or something, after a while she was able to explain to Dan what really happened in Matt room.

 Dan got angry with her because they agreed that no more Matt or anyone. Dan even ask Barack if she was having doubts about them and is really Matt she wanted, and she was just settling for him because Matt was giving her a cold shoulder.

She left without responding, and Dan quickly followed her, and he stopped her from walking and he asked her if she was sad that Matt fell into sin or she was sad because of jealousy .she didn't answer again.

He said henceforth he forbid her from going to Matt room for any reason.

Faith Without Fruit is Dead

After two weeks she finally saw Matt however he was like a total stranger he was still hurting and very angry with her, so he never gave her a chance to talk to him, just hello and he kept on walking.

Luckily for both of them, Matt was preparing his final exam, and he was done with his degree and after the exam, Matt was leaving the school for good.

So it was hard for him to even look at both of them so leaving for good after exam was working to his advantage.

After the exam, he bought a book of -battle of the mind by Joyce Meyer - and gave it to one of his friends to give it to Barack as he heard that Dan doesn't want him around Barack anymore.

So he respected that and stayed away, Dan was also in his final year however he still had six months to complete while Barack was still in her second year.

Matt got a job on one of Petroleum Company which was 350 km south of the Gauteng province, six months later Dan completed as well, unfortunately Dan as well got a job 400km North of Gauteng but his advantage was, and where he was working was only 75km away from Barack village.

So it was easy for her to visit him on school holidays. Dan also meets the local Pastor of Barack church in the village, and he also met Barack family.

Faith Without Fruit is Dead

After they all left Barack continued with a legacy Matt thought her, she was going very strong in her walk with the Lord and also in leading the prayer warriors.

She never stopped to pray for Matt even though they were not communicating and she didn't even have his number anymore, Matt tried to move on with his life but all his relationship were not working as he was always comparing every girl he dated with Barack eventually they all dumped him.

Chapter 4

Distance relationships didn't work for Dan and Barack.

Dan as well wasn't good in keeping distance relationship , his weakness also got the better of him when he started befriending the girls of the church he was fellowshipping ,one of them happened to be his colleague who invited him to fellowship with them ,they were always together at work ,church and also doing the same church activities and were becoming closer , the more they spend time together the more he forgot to call Barack, because Barack was also busy with church and school activities ,they didn't notice the gap between them again, when Barack completed Dan persuaded her to move back home so that she can look for a job in the same town he was working so that they should work on their relationship and be close again, it made sense at the time so she agreed ,but the longer it took Barack to get a job the more frustrated she got and the more they didn't see each other as she was not able to afford to visit him every day or every weekend, Barack family was still poor and they were also hoping that she will get a job soon and help her siblings too with school fees.

Faith Without Fruit is Dead

It took Barack the whole year to find a job until she decides not to be choosey and look for a job anywhere, Dan also realize that he has been selfish not considering her family background.

He allowed her to look for a job wherever she may find it, and she will come back after they got married, their plans was for Barack to get a job and work for six months then they will plan for their wedding.

Barack got an offer to do interns at the bank in their sales department in Pretoria which was not far from Matt home. It was one year internship, then after they complete they will be offered a permanent position, Barack took the offer and hoping that after a year, Barack will ask to be transferred in a town which Dan was working, it was a perfect plan but little did they know that the Lord had answered Matt prayer 2yrs ago but he was just waiting for the perfect time.

Barack moved back to Gauteng province to work as an intern, Dan and his colleague they compromised their faith soon after Barack went back to Pretoria and she got pregnant within a month.

Barack didn't qualify to take a vacation leave for 4months, after Easter she was given 4days leave, so she decided to take a taxi and head straight to Dan's house to surprise him.

She arrived there around 2pm only to find a 4months pregnant lady in Dan house wearing his shirt, and she fainted and that lady called ambulance for her and at the hospital, Dan new girlfriend registered Barack with a name of Dan sister and she even called Dan to come home as his sister was

Faith Without Fruit is Dead

admitted in hospital, Dan drove straight to hospital and when he got into a ward he found his new pregnant girlfriend sitting next to his girlfriend of almost 2yrs.

He turned very fast hoping they didn't see him unfortunately they both did as Barack was also awake, they called him and when he got into a room Barack was just crying , the only word she spoke was please bring my bag so that I can take a taxi to go home, he tried to insist that he can drive her home but she knew how awkward it was going to be so she refused, Dan went home, brought her bags ,Barack was discharged after 4pm and she got a taxi to go back to Gauteng province ,she wanted to be alone . But before Dan gave her – her bags he wrote an apology letter and also to explained what happened, when he was giving her a letter she gave him his ring back and said "I see that these now belong to someone else" and those words were like a sword to Dan's heart as he never intended to hurt Barack. But because the child was one the way he had to bear the responsibility and let go of Barack.

Now to Barack it looked like God didn't found her worthy to marry the two best friend she ever had, as both of them found solicit in another woman's arm, it looked like her keeping her innocent was becoming a curse as the people she kept herself for they were gone.

She blamed herself for everything and she even confess that she drove the good man to commit what they would have never committed if they never met her.

Faith Without Fruit is Dead

Barack spend week without eating even water tasted bitter to her, on Monday when she got to work, she was a mess and her team leader thought that maybe someone closed to her dead and she didn't tell them, in afternoon she collapsed and was rushed to a hospital and the doctor told her team leader that Barack was suicidal and since there was no close family member closed by after they discharged her, her team leader took her straight to her own house.

Barack team leader is none other than Matt's mother however at home they call him Nkateko which means blessing, Barack after some days she told Matt mom about Dan and what lead to their break up and she also told her and Jay – Matt younger brother about her life at University including her friendship with Matt and how they got separated.

Barack lived with them and they offered her an outside flat which happened to be Matt flat which he built when he started working so that he can have a holiday house in his parents' house since they don't have quest room.

Because Matt was not in the country around that time, they accommodate Barack, because she removed all Matt item like picture Barack never notice that Nkateko and Matt are the same people.

Barack was the best cook better than Matt 's mother , most of the time Barack cooked for the family and Matt dad taught Barack some of his old recipes, he even said jokily after seeing that Barack used the recipes ,he said that since she learned his family secret recipes the best she can do to thank him was to marry one of his sons, Jay even laugh and said " I hope that son should be me," the truth was Jay was 6months younger than Barack so besides the fact that she doesn't trust man anymore Jay was just too young for her .

Every day she was thinking about finding Matt and even on the family prayer meeting she will be unconscious pray for him loudly while praying with Matt family. She stayed with them for 6 months every time she wanted to leave and go back to her old flat, they refused because they were now used to having her around, she was like a daughter they never had especially since they didn't have a daughter, they even said if marriage doesn't work then they will just adopt her as long as she will continue to be part of their life.

Matt and Barack got second chance.

Six months later on Friday Matt came back from Singapore and since he got engage before he left, he told his family not to come and fetch him as his fiancé was and he was expecting his fiancé to meet him at the airport.

Barack helped to prepare his favorite meal; Barack used to cook for Matt at school so she was familiar with the meal and she gave it her best.

Matt waited at the airport for long until it was late as he was longing to see his fiancé and he thought maybe he made mistake with time .because his line was still on roaming at the airport he couldn't call her and after hours he borrowed a phone of one of taxi man so that he can call her still she didn't answer. He took a taxi straight to her house when he got there he was told that she went on the date with someone she has been seen for the past 4months.

Faith Without Fruit is Dead

He was devastated, meanwhile back home everyone was waiting for him with anticipation, and when it got late he called them to tell them not to worry he was on his way, at that time Barack went to her room, she didn't want to stay till late because she was working on Saturday's.

So when he finally arrived they were so happy as it has been months since they saw him, he told them stories and they told him stories of the new additional member in the family and Jay kept on saying Barack is a sister he always wanted while Matt parents kept referring Barack as the daughter they always wanted.

The more they told him her background, the more the story sound familiar, they stayed until 3am, just before they went to sleep Matt mom said Dan and Matt really damaged the faith of Barack in men.

 Matt asked his mom to repeat the name of a new boyfriend and old boyfriend, she said his name is Matt" again "and Matt asked have you seen him", they all said no they lost touch while they were still at school and they haven't spoke for the past 3yrs.

By then Matt was on his feet taking out his wallet from his back pocket, and he took out a small piece of paper, and he gave it to his mom. Out of shock, she threw it away.

Jay knowing how his mom was afraid of snake even when they are on paper he took it and looked at it thinking it might be a snake, Matt father notice Jay went into a trance as well he took the picture from his hand.

Faith Without Fruit is Dead

Matt kept saying is it her,? Is it her and no one was able to answer, Matt dad fell back on his couch because that picture was of the lady they were telling Matt about and he has her picture and his dad asked who send you this picture, did your too forward mother send you this picture,?

She woke up from her trance said never, I never even thought of doing that, or even mentioned Barack to him before now.

Finally their dreams were about to come true, Matt said to his dad do you remember these picture, he said "I don't but I know that girl", Matt said "3 yrs. ago we bought a ring for a girl I met at university and you advised me to ask God 1st before I proposed consequently someone else proposed to her", they all went aaaahhhaah, it was her ?They asked, Matt said yes and he asked: "is the woman in the picture the same girl with your Barack."

They couldn't find words to answer him, Matt stood up out of frustration as no one was able to answer him; he started shaking his younger brother Jay to talk, and Jay screamed " yes yes yes she is the same person. You're Barack, and our Barack is the same person.

And she has been sleeping in your bed since you left."

Matt wanted to go and knock at her door, but his dad said "that is not a good idea and consequence might be fatal, be a gentleman and approached her nicely tomorrow when she come back from work, right now go to sleep because tomorrow might be a big day for you. The day you missed 3 yrs. ago so you need to rest"

Faith Without Fruit is Dead

Matt wondered what kind of a weird coincidence was that; he became afraid and excited at the same time; everyone finally went to sleep off their shock as well.

Matt remembered all the nasty things he did and said against God after he lost Barack to Dan.

In the morning Matt woke his mother up so that she will call Barack, she asked Jay instead to ask Barack to pass by the main house before she leaves for work.

After 6:30am Barack was done and ready to go to work and she knocked at the kitchen door, Jay ushered her to the living room where everyone except Matt was standing and waiting in anticipation of her reaction when she finally met Matt. She greeted them, and no one responded.

Matt was sitting on the couch which she was standing behind it, so she didn't recognize him from behind; Matt mother said I called you so that you may meet my son Nkateko

, Barack said oh with a voice of excitement, he is here?

Before his mom can respond, he stood up and turns to face Barack.

Barack stood there with her mouth opened while everything was falling from her hands slowing and she almost followed them to the ground luckily Jay was still standing next to her, Jay helped her to set down.

No one was talking Barack, and Matt eye were filled with tears,

Faith Without Fruit is Dead

Matt parents and Jay's eyes were moving between them; Matt finally held Barack hand to help her stood up to embraced him.

She hugged him and she broke down and cry as the flashback of her old life with Matt was moving like slides in her mind, they stood there and embraced each other for a while with tears running down their eyes, eventually Matt parents and Jay left them alone.

All Matt could say to her was I am sorry, I am here now, everything will be alright, he was just saying those words but really he didn't even understand why Barack broke down like that .it just reminded him of the 1st day he spoke to her under the shade next to a SCF and studio when he was singing for her.

Matt said to Barack "I still can't believe that this time I met you in my parent living room" God has a big sense of humor, he just wants to prove that he is God and he can do anything, anytime.

He brought you back to me and put you in my bed what is he saying? Matt already heard so much about Barack in the last 10hours from his family.

Barack on the other hand is aware that he is engaged because Matt mom often spoke about how she missed her son Nkateko and how she was looking forward to plan his wedding once he comes back.

Matt after a while he stood up and went to the store room where his mother said she kept all his thing , he came back few minutes later with the ring he once bought for Barack, Matt promised himself last night that he wasn't going to hesitate like 3yrs ago to propose to Barack, he already heard that she was available and looking for him , God with his big sense humor delivered Barack into his home as a sign that he approve ,all that looks like it was a hand written on the wall confirming that they belong together.

Matt finally got a chance propose.

He kneeled down and said "3yrs ago I bought these ring for you, while I was praying for it another man snatched you and I heard that he let you go and God of all the homes in this town he brought you in my house to show you where you belong, and I heard that my parents wish to adopt you but I am glad that they couldn't otherwise it was going to be awkward for me to marry my own sister, so will you please be my wife please, it took us 3yrs to be where we are now , in that three yrs. I have been with other woman and none of them make me feel the way I feel when I am with you, I carried you in my heart and your picture in my wallet as I reminder of who I am, to remind myself of the man inside me. You are my better half, please spend the rest of your life with me" by then tears was running down their eyes, Barack slowly and shaking she stretched out her hand to towards Matt to put a ring on her figure however she pause and pull back her hand. Matt asked again will you be my wife?

Barack hesitated, the voice in her head was telling her that Matt is engaged and the other voice was saying he is meant for you, Barack took the ring from Matt's hands but she didn't wear it ,neither did she said anything to Matt, she took her bag a run out of the house to catch a taxi as she was late for work.

Matt mom and Jay when they hear the sound of the door closing, they came back; Matt was still kneeling down, holding an empty box.

His mom said, "did she accept?"

Matt while crying said she didn't say no or yes, neither did she wore the ring, Matt was scared that Barack is going to reject him again. He was so devastated, he said his father who was trying to calm him down "these can't happen again, I won't survive it, I won't, please do something.

Matt dad said to him delay is not denial, she is still in shock, you had 6 hours of processing these, and you expect her to process it in 6munites? "

Matt dad said to him "our God is an intentional God and he never fail, so all what has happened between you, God has made it work for your good. For him to bring her here is his way of saying he is in control and all things are possible with him, don't give up now"

The bank closed at 11am and 10:30 Matt was already waiting for her outside.

Barack when she got to work she went to the bathroom and looked at a ring. She put it on just to see if it was still a fit and when she try to remove it, she couldn't she put a hand soup try to make her figure to be slippery but it was still stuck, she kept saying, no no no he is engaged I can't do to another woman what Dan has done to me, I can't is not right, please, please ring get off my figure please. She used everything to pull out the ring, but it was still stuck. She even prayed, but her prayer wasn't answered as it was a wrong prayer.

After work when she approached Matt, he noticed that she was wearing the ring, he was relieved but didn't say anything, when they got home she asked about his fiancé and he told her what had happened, but she didn't believe him.

She said well your ring is stuck on me, I was admiring it and also wondering how it will look on me, and I put and it on, it got stuck so some reason.

They found Matt dad and mom in the living area, and they asked her if she accepted his proposal, Barack looked at them for a while, her heart wanted to say yes, but her mind said, he is lying he is still engaged.

She sit down and shake her head; then she said to Matt mom " mother didn't you said your Nkateko is engaged and planning to get married as soon as he comes back home, is Matt that Nkateko .Matt mom sobbed too and said yes it true he was engaged but we just learned that that engagement was broken yesterday that's why Nkateko came home so late, and I even called her to find out if it is true fortunately she agreed to talk to me and explained to me why she couldn't wait for him to come back.

It turn out that before Matt went away, his other girlfriend bought him a wallet as going away gift and she took out all the item on the old wallet to put them on the new wallet she just bought and among them was a picture of Matt and Barack and when she asked Matt about the picture Matt lied and said she was his cousin and she was late.

And the day Matt arrived with Barack from hospital, she recognized her and asked Matt mom who the lady was and she was told she is Barack and her colleague.so she didn't believe that they don't know her and that's when she decided to leave Matt because she finally meet the girl he was always telling her about in his own house with his mother, she felt betrayed. That the story of how the engagement was called off.

Matt mom and dad kneeled before Barack, and she jumped from the couch as she never saw what they were about to do being done anywhere.

They asked her to marry their son Nkateko, she looked at them for a while and she kneeled before them as well to embrace them while they were all still kneeling and she said I will marry him, Matt came closer and kneel next to Barack and prayer broke off and they were all praying thanking God, Jay went into the kitchen and he came with a leftover red wine and he pour on top of them and circling it around them, why he did that nobody knows.

Jay also played a song of -his is intentional by-Travis Greene- and they celebrated just 5 of them the engagement, 3months later Barack and Matt got married.